Albatros

To Dad with Love

Lucie Hášová Truhelková
Illustrated by Andrea Tachezy

Grandad's Pink Trousers

Albatros

Once upon a time,
there was an old man.

He frowned often, didn't like people much,
and people didn't really like him.

He never bought roses
for his wife on her birthday.

Even though he knew
this made her sad.

He never allowed anyone to drain the bathtub until he filled two large buckets with the water.

He kept the buckets of water next
to the toilet for flushing.
When visitors came, his wife felt ashamed.

After he took out the trash, he brought back
the plastic bin bag and returned it to the bin.

Even though he knew that the bag was smelly and that his wife was disgusted by it.

Whenever his wife asked what he wanted
for dinner, his answer was the same:

"I'll eat what needs to be eaten."

If he happened to find out that she had
thrown away an out-of-date yogurt,
he would get angry.

When his wife asked him to take
old clothes to the sorted waste container,
he didn't do it.

Instead, he took the clothes to his garage
and went through them again.

Once, he found some old pink trousers of his
wife's that were no longer in fashion, and he put
them on.

He wore them to the baker's and to the newsstand.

Because of the trousers, people laughed
at him behind his back. His wife was mortified.

One morning, as the man in the pink trousers was returning from the shops, his phone rang.

He took the call, listened for a moment, and then burst into tears. A little boy had just been born. His grandchild.

From that day on, people would see the man in the pink trousers in the street with a stroller.

He and the little boy would take their walk at noon.

Every day. Come rain, frost, snow, or whatever.

The grandad in the pink trousers pushed the stroller with great care. He chatted to the little boy the whole time, and he never stopped smiling.

After the grandson grew too big for the stroller, the old man in the pink trousers would walk slowly along the path, with the unsteady little boy clinging to his hand, and they would talk and talk.

Once, when the boy was a little older, he looked up at the man and asked, "Grandad, why are you nice to me and grumpy to others?"

The man was taken aback.
"Why don't you buy roses for Grandma?"
the boy asked.

"Why does she have to flush with water
from a bucket? And why don't you let her
throw away those old trousers?"

The man thought before answering.
"It's like this," he said at last.
"Those roses travel halfway across the world
to our shops. That's bad for the climate.

And the growers treat them with a special spray
to make them look fresh longer. This spray makes
people who live nearby seriously ill."

"What flows when we flush our toilet is drinking water. Yet, there are lots of people in the world who don't have enough water to drink."

"When I think about it like that,
I can't flush it away.
That's why I pour in the water
we've already used."

"The bags we put our trash in are made of plastic.
After we throw them away, they stay where we leave them.

Once, when I was driving past a huge dump,
I saw thin pieces of plastic floating above it like ghosts.
The wind was blowing them into the woods and the fields.

It takes many years for this plastic
to decompose and disappear."

"I'd like everyone in the world to have a fridge filled with food. But for every one of us here who has more yogurt, cheese, and meat than we can eat, on the other side of the world there's someone whose tummy is empty.

I just can't throw away a yogurt two days past its sell-by date, when I know that there are people who would give all they have for it."

"As for these trousers I'm wearing, they may have been made by a little boy of about your age who was working in a factory to earn money for his family.

If I threw them away, Grandma would buy me another pair. I don't want more trousers made that way." The little boy thought about all this. "I see," he said.

"Now I understand, Grandad. But I couldn't do what you do. I wouldn't like it if other people thought that I was grumpy and silly."

The old man in the pink trousers looked
at his grandson for a moment before answering.

"What strangers think about you isn't important.
All that matters is the opinion of the one
you're doing it for. Your grandson."

GRANDAD'S PINK TROUSERS
Lucie Hášová Truhelková
Illustrated by Andrea Tachezy

Layout design and typesetting: Daniela Danielová
Translation: Andrew Oakland
Coordination: Veronika Kopečková

© Albatros Media Group, 2022.
5. května 1746/22, Prague 4, Czech Republic.
Printed in China by Leo Paper Group.

978-80-00-06592-2